REX

By

Oliver Franklin

BUDDLEWOOD HOUSE

Contents

1. A Climbing Boy's Lot...1

2. Three Disparate Visitors....................................13

3. Audience with the Detective..............................23

4. Matchboxes and Scandal.....................................35

5. A Tragic Ending..49

6. Burgled!...57

7. The Villainous Dr Coote....................................71

8. Albert's Fate..82

9. The Abandoned..92

10. Inheritance...101

This is the "true" *Mr Arthur's Toyshop,* parts of which Septimus reads in his second adventure. However the bulk of this book was written after the fact and should the reader notice any discrepancies, please overlook them.

REX

Chapter 1

A Climbing Boy's Lot

The yellow smog was descending upon Oxford Street, late in the afternoon as the hustle-bustle and clatter of hooves surged all around him like a great swell of the river. Meanwhile the young boy in cap and jacket was transfixed by the scene beyond the window. A myriad of colour and shape overwhelmed his senses and, were it not for the burgeoning signs of Christmas elsewhere, this oasis of joy would have appeared so out of place, as to be quite unreal. The panes of spun glass, with all their imperfection turned a clockwork soldier into a broken rainbow, a coloured lantern into a cascade of jewels and the man behind the counter into a many-headed monster.

With his face pressed up against the window, Rex didn't notice the other man approaching.

'You want to be getting home, Son, asides 't'll be dark soon!'

Rex turned and saw the lamplighter going about his business, albeit if the smog were really heavy, the lamps were neither fit for man nor beast. Still, he had a job to do.

'I have no home, Sir,' Rex replied.

'Oh – well – don't be loitering. Folk'll think you're up to no good,' and he continued on his way, stopping at intervals and leaving another orange glow behind him. Soon he disappeared from view amongst the crowds, but the telltale balls of flame gave away his presence for a long time after.

Being cold and having spent nearly the whole day searching for board and lodging, and being determined not to return to the workhouse, Rex decided this was his last chance before heading back to find a place under the bridge, or in a cellar. In truth he had little experience of life on the street, but had learned by what he'd seen and heard of others. Mr Watkin had at least had the heart to warn him not to fall foul of the Poor Laws, before turning him out of his house. Rex didn't know much about the law but he knew only too well the grim regime of the workhouse. And spending the next five years of his life as a climbing boy, in comparison was positively pleasant. He had even been taught to read – a rare delight for someone of his status. In fact the London Society of Master Sweeps operated under a set code, which included the exemption from working on the Sabbath and the obligation to attend Sunday school in order to study and learn to read the bible.

Climbing boys were kept in some harsh conditions, often sleeping in cellars, their beds nothing more than bags of soot. But Rex would take that job any day of the week rather than the horrors of the treadmill, seeing exhausted colleagues fall from the wheel to be crushed in the works.

Concerning the apprenticeship of workhouse children, originally, boys had to be aged from ten to eighteen years old, to undertake an apprenticeship. However with the passing of the Parish Apprentices Act of 1698, the allowable age of entry was reduced to seven. Rex had been indentured at the earliest opportunity but a growth spurt at the age of twelve had put pay to that, along with his master's retirement. Mr Watkin had been a smaller operator, employing only three boys, the two other of which had died through soot on the lungs. And now that Rex had outgrown the chimneys, he had been released from his servitude, put out of the house with some money in his hand and told to find his own way.

So here he was, with one last roll of the dice. Trembling, he pushed open the door. The bell chimed and he made his way inside.

The dusty stillness of the shop was in stark contrast to the clamour of the street but he scarcely had time to enjoy the scene. All at once a sharp voice boomed out, 'What do you want, boy?'

Rex looked up and saw a man in a cloth cap and apron with half-moon spectacles balanced on the tip of his nose. He was sporting whiskers and looked to be in his mid-to-late fifties. He was standing behind the counter with a toy steam engine in one hand and a dirty rag in the other.

'P-Please sir, I am a poor boy looking for work.'

'A beggar?' the man snapped, replacing the toy on the counter and leaning forwards a little to examine him.

'N-No, Sir, I have have money. I am lately released from my master's service and am looking for another apprenticeship.'

'Your master, you say? Of what trade was he? You are certainly very young to be freed. So answer me particularly; were you dismissed for pilfering?'

4

'Not so, but I was a climbing boy. My master retired and I outgrew the chimneys.'

'How old are you in truth?'

'Twelve, Sir.'

And soon it was altogether clear that this boy was neither a liar nor a thief and after somewhat more questioning Mr William Arthur, the shopkeeper who, as it happened, had been contemplating taking on a boy for some months, found himself well disposed towards the lad. Indeed, only the day before he had discussed the matter with his wife and suggested they approach the workhouse in search of a suitable candidate. Not so much as to prepare for their future but rather to accommodate the Christmas season. But would they find a candidate more suitable than this? The boy could read and write, follow instructions and had the wits to survive a cruel station for a number of years. Maybe the winds of fate had cast this lonely leaf through his door on their breeze? Or as a good Christian man should cite – the manifest providence of God.

'...and unlike the others, I had a mind to always hold my breath and I became quite good at it. I could last several minutes. So my lungs didn't fill with soot and—'

The shopkeeper held up his hand to silence Rex in the midst of recounting all his doings and said, 'Very well! I shall give you a trial, board and lodging – just until the New Year. If you do well, come January we may keep you on and pay you wages. Otherwise, you're on your way. Agreed?'

'Thank you most kindly, Sir!' Rex said and bowed deeply.

Mr Arthur ran the shop together with his wife and Rex was soon after to meet her in the scullery where, having surveyed him with interest and checked his teeth ('As with the teeth, so with the bones!') she provided him a bowl of slop and two slices of bread. The scullery was behind the shop and in the corner of the room there were stairs leading down to the cellar. Upstairs there was a large workshop and a small bedroom, where the master and mistress retired so there was no place for the boy except on a straw mattress under the counter.

That night Rex went to bed fully dressed and as he settled down under a blanket that was barely adequate, he watched the red glow from the stove grow dimmer and dimmer and considered his lot was not so bad after all. What else could it be? Surely this was preferable to the cruelty of the workhouse, the ever-present danger of the slum or the deathly cold of an abandoned hulk on the riverbank?

The next morning life in the street seemed to begin while it was still dark. He awoke to the rattle of a cart, a shout and the clatter of hooves, for what was evidently the neighbours' coal delivery. When they were replenished the cart pulled up directly outside the shop and Rex could hear the horses' breath. The lid of the coal hole was pulled up and then came a rumble as a black torrent poured into the cellar. Then the lid was replaced and the cart moved on. Rex looked over at the wall but could not make out the time on the clock. Though he heard the chimes not long after and knew it to be five. He felt he had barely fallen asleep again only to to hear his name called out and a wooden spoon banging on a pan. It was the mistress.

'Rex! Look lively! Make up the fire while I get the breakfast.'

Rex wondered whether he ought not wash his face first and make himself presentable but he considered that the order had been to help the mistress with the fire, so he proceeded from the room. He was good with fires, having worked with a sweep and had often been charged with making up a small fire so the master could tell whether the chimney was drawing or not. And sometimes it wasn't, as all manner of foreign objects had found their way into chimneys, including, on one occasion a dead crow. Whether the unfortunate bird had succumbed to the smoke or was dead when it fell in, nobody knew but it did a fine job of blocking the draft.

Rex had a lively blaze going in five minutes and as the mistress meant to keep the stove all day he fetched a scuttle of coal up from the cellar. He filled the grate and soon it glowed bright orange and warmed the whole room. Meanwhile the mistress, still in her nightdress and gown, was cutting up some bacon. She turned and passed Rex a copper kettle.

'Set that on, boy! You and I shall have a cup of tea. Whereas Mr Arthur is of a more traditional bent and prefers his shot of gin to start the day.' Seeing the boy make a face, she added, 'Ye might grin, but in the old days they used to tax tea at double so only the high and mighty could afford it. That's why we common folk drank gin, you see? Then the government lowered the tax and so everyone could drink it. Much better if you ask me.'

'Yes, Miss,' Rex agreed. 'I had no idea how tea came to be common.'

Mr Arthur came downstairs at seven and they took breakfast together. This struck Rex as strange in that, every other place he had lived and laboured, those in authority and their charges ate separately – as did rulers and slaves since antiquity. After breakfast, at his mistress's bidding Rex took some warm water from an urn on the stove and washed his hands and face in a bowl on the table. The working day began at eight o'clock when he ventured outside with the master to help with the shutters. Then it was up to the workshop to assist before opening at nine.

From the sporadic signs of life many hours earlier, to the time they came downstairs and unlocked the door, Oxford Street had become a portrait brimming with life and motion. If this was the meaning of passing trade, there was certainly plenty of it passing. Numerous faces peered in through the window including, Rex was quick to notice, faces younger than his own.

'We do sell to customers who collect,' Mr Arthur began, 'but most folk are placing orders for Christmas. So we will have a good deal of deliveries to make. And I shall need you to mind the shop on occasion when Mrs Arthur is out too.'

'Yes, Sir,' Rex obliged.

'For the present, make up the stove. My fingers are that cold I can hardly feel them! Then come and see how I keep the ledger.'

Upon reading the leather tome Rex immediately saw his advantage over others in terms of employment in knowing numbers and letters. For the ledger contained both and it was not hard to understand, though it took him a good deal more effort in working out the correct money to return to the customers. Whereas the master seemed to reckon the amount in moments, as though he had everything in his head afore time.

'Do not trouble yourself,' the shopkeeper said. 'In time you too shall have it all in your head.'

'All of it?' Rex repeated, staring wide-eyed at the multitude of colourful objects on the shelves, each with it's own price and the numbers to work out afterwards.

A handful of people came in that morning and about luncheon, they noticed a boy standing close by the shop with a large tray strapped around his shoulders. He had been at his station some time and, despite his coat and hat,

Rex noticed the lad appeared to be shivering in the cold. With his master's grace he ventured outside and enquired of the same.

'Would you care for an apple, Master?' the boy asked as he approached. 'I have Blenheim Orange and Coxes Orange Pippin.'

'Apples in winter?' Rex asked, most curious.

'Yes, Master, we keep them on a bed of straw in the cellar, not touching each other. So if any go bad, they won't taint t'other. In the cold they may last until New Year and even longer,' the boy explained.

'I never knew,' Rex murmured, as he read the lettering around the edge of the tray – Edwin Cummins and Co. Fruiterers. 'Three Coxes please,' he said, feeling in his pocket for some pennies. 'You look cold, can I bring you a hot drink of tea?'

The boy was a year or two younger than Rex and upon hearing this, his face lit up. 'Bless you, yes please!'

Rex took the fruit in a paper bag and went back into the shop. 'It is the fruiterer's boy, he sold me some apples,' he explained, showing his master the bag. 'He is so very cold out there, may I take him a pot of tea?'

'I suppose,' the shopkeeper grunted. 'Better yet, make us all a drink and we shall have those apples for supper if you please.'

The apple seller, who turned out to be the owner of the auspicious name of Albert, came by the toyshop for the next few days and he and Rex struck up a friendship, which soon resulted in hot drinks gratis and apples likewise. And thereafter Albert introduced Rex to his particular friend Lavender Braithwaite who was standing on the corner opposite selling matches in handmade boxes. The pair of them often smiled at one another through the crowd and Rex had the impression they imagined they loved one another.

Chapter 2

Three Disparate Visitors

The first week in the toyshop passed by quickly and throughout Rex felt that his position was a safe one, at least until January. Certainly he was never threatened or abused and the Arthurs appeared to be satisfied with his work and manners. His appearance had also been the cause of some comment from customers who were used only to seeing William and Mary Arthur behind the counter. And now Rex had two new friends of his own age (his old friends being mostly dead) and with them came the prospect of gaining more.

On the following Monday morning, after a glorious bath in front of the scullery stove, his first in over a week and a half, Rex was charged with minding the shop while his master made a delivery and the mistress worked about the house and yard. So from nine o'clock he had the oversight and was keen to show himself up to the task.

The first half-hour was quiet but then a man with a cart pulled up outside, squinted through the window and pushed open the door. The bell chimed and the man shuffled inside, leaving the handcart in the doorway with a cage and various other items on board. He was short, stout and very round-shouldered, barely taller than Rex himself. He wore a flat cap, smock and leather boots and carried a mangy cat under his arm. When he spoke it was with an affected air though Rex could tell he was no gentleman as the fellow did not remove his cap indoors.

'Good morning, young master!'

'Good morning, Sir. How can I help?'

'I am 'ere to offer me services, to yourself an' your neighbours asides.'

'Services?' Rex repeated, looking around to see if the mistress happened to be nearby but she was evidently in the yard. Less the gentleman, rather more the costermonger, it seemed. 'What kind of services, Sir?'

'I'm a rat-catcher by trade, see? This 'ere is Spike – ' he stroked the cat under its scruffy neck ' – he's the scourge of

14

the vermin in the city. Got an 'undred and fifty of 'em in his time 'e 'as an' no word of a lie!'

Rex stared at the beast – bedraggled and sorrowful, with patches of fur missing and doubted whether it was fit for catching anything. Then he said, 'The master is away on his round delivering to customers' houses. He shall be back presently. Shall I call the mistress? Though I doubt that we need a rat-catcher. This street is clear, I think.'

'That's what they all says, Sir, but sooner or later they knows better. We sees to that!' Then, noticing the boy's innocence and confusion he drew near and continued in a whisper. 'Let me show you a trade secret. Often times a client says they don't need me services, don't they? So I bids them good day and makes me way. Then, later on I lets loose a couple of the vermin from me cage over their wall an', guess what? When I comes by the week following they changes their tune and offers me a job after all.'

Rex was aghast at the man's corrupt practise but feared to speak out as he found the fellow quite intimidating. However something of his thoughts must have shown on his face because the man barked, 'What you gawpin' at?'

Rex started backwards and mumbled, 'N–Nothing, Sir.'

'You bein' a shopkeeper an' all! You oughter know, there ain't nothin' more important than a satisfied customer. Nothin'! You do what you 'ave to to keep the client 'appy! An' 'ere's another thing. Spike, well, 'e's gettin' old now and don't always gets the beast in question and sometimes poison don't work neither. Nor yet me traps! So I gets one of them dead ones from me cage out there and shows it to the customer. Then 'e's 'appy and pays up, an' I'm 'appy and everything carries on just lovely.'

By now Rex had heard quite enough to know this fellow to be an out and out crook. Summoning up all his courage he said, 'Sir, thank you for your time but I really don't think we need your services. But if you insist, I may go and call the mistress?'

His offer of his calling the mistress seemed to effect the man in the shop as it had been a threat and, saying a begrudging 'Good day' he shuffled out again, took up the handle of his cart and trundled away. Rex frowned as he watched the man disappearing into the throng. Is this how the rat-catchers always operated? Or was this fellow a lone criminal in an otherwise honest trade? He supposed time would tell.

A short while afterwards the doorbell rang again and a bustling, middle-aged woman came in, looking somewhat flustered and out of breath. Her silver hair was tied up in a tight bun and her bonnet and dress were of the same dour grey. She wore a thick shawl and comforter and promptly remarked how good it was to be in the warm. Her accent was marked and certainly not from London. Rex couldn't place it but guessed at somewhere North where all the dialects were strange.

'Can I help you, Madam?'

'Oh, yes, I do hope so! Now I don't have long but, anyway, it's my great-nephew, you see? I wish to get him a special present for Christmas. His parents are in reduced circumstances and I would like to make up for it.'

'How old is he, Ma'am? As you see we have a range of toys and games for children,' Rex replied, turning and gesturing to the array of wares behind him. Meanwhile he was anxiously rehearsing numbers in his head.

'Five – no, tell a lie, he is six - but here's the thing: he says he wants a toy locomotive. Do you have any such thing?'

Rex scratched his head and began searching the shelves. There was a painted, wooden train and also a tin steam engine. He brought these down for her inspection and placed them on the counter. She was undoubtedly impressed but rather particular.

'I was hoping for something bigger, something he can ride on if need be. Can you make me one like this – ' she indicated the locomotive from the train set ' - except bigger and brightly coloured?'

The master undertakes all manner of bespoke work,' Rex answered, 'I am sure he can provide exactly what you want. It may take him a few days but I venture it will be ready by Friday.'

'Excellent! Shall I pay now?' she asked.

'Ah – the master usually takes a deposit – a shilling, I think,' Rex answered, fetching a pencil and leaf of paper. May I take your name and address, Ma'am?'

'Mrs Hudson, of 221 Baker Street,' she obliged, opening her purse.

'Baker Street?' Rex mused, scribbling away on the paper, 'I have heard of such a place, though I have not been there.'

'Will that be all, Master?' Mrs Hudson asked, handing him the coin.

'I think so,' said Rex. 'We look forward to seeing you again Friday, or should we deliver the parcel to you?'

'Deliver it, please,' she replied and with that, hurried out of the shop upon other business.

Rex was left feeling windswept by her brisk manner but also pleased to have taken his first commission. He placed the shilling carefully in the money box and signed his name on the order, grinning. And yet, before the hour was up he spotted Albert outside again with his tray of apples and he thought to put the kettle on the stove but then another gentleman came into the shop. This fellow wore a mackintosh and leather gloves. He exuded a professional air and stepped smartly up to the counter and presented Rex with his calling card. "Havelock Watkins-Rhymes – the Times Newspaper – junior correspondent" it read.

Rex was perplexed. 'Ah – can I help you, Sir?'

'Quite possibly, young man,' he replied jovially. 'I am from the Times as you see and I am researching the life of the underclass in London. Our readers are simply fascinated with the day-to-day doings of the slum, especially its moral life and I am hoping to conduct interviews with those who have first-hand knowledge of the subject.'

Rex was still bemused. 'This is Oxford Street, Sir, and most folk hereabouts are well to do, I think. There are some well known places I've heard of – Devil's Acre, Old Nichol or in the other direction there's Pottery Lane. I've never been to those places but if you would like me to direct you to—'

'No need, my man,' the reporter interrupted. 'It is easy for our readers to think of the inhabitants of the slums not so much in terms of hard-working yet poor, rather idle, drunkards and thieves. For example it is reported that Field Lane, in Clerkenwell is occupied entirely by receivers of stolen goods, which are openly spread out for sale. The police have excused their lack of intervention by arguing that the place is too dangerous to enter, but I am a reporter not an enforcer of the law and I mean to get to the bottom of the matter.'

'I am not sure how I can help,' Rex admitted.

'I would just ask that you keep my card in your possession and should you hear of any—'

But he himself was interrupted as Mr Arthur returned at that instant. And seeing the fellow he immediately took charge.

'How can I help you, Sir?'

There was something about the master's abrupt arrival and brusque address that caused this latest visitor to falter. In the pause that followed, Rex answered for the man.

'This is a reporter from the Times, Master, he is seeking interviews.'

At these words the atmosphere in the room changed and the two men eyed one another with reservation. The silence was ultimately broken by Mr Watkins-Rhymes who remarked, 'Thank you for your time and keep the card! I'll be on my way.' And without another word he left the shop.

'Egregious fellow,' the shopkeeper muttered. 'What can his business here be? Tell me, child, did he ask you any questions?'

Rex shook his head. 'No, Sir, we barely had the time. You arrived directly after him. Why? Are you suspicious of him?'

'Indeed,' the master replied, shaking off his cloak. 'Have you ever read the scandalous material some of his ilk write? It's enough to turn your head.'

Rex shook his head. 'I thought they told the news,' he said.

'In part, they do but 'tis all the gossip and slander they add to it that makes for the problem.'

However the shopkeeper was well pleased with the locomotive commission and upon hearing the address of the client, was greatly affected. He wouldn't tell Rex quite why he felt so elated but instead went to inform his wife while Rex made tea and took a pot out to Albert and they beckoned Lavender come and join them. She obliged and they drank and chatted together while the people passed by about their business.

Chapter 3

Audience with the Detective

The group of boys hurrying up the street were dressed in caps, boots and jackets and ranged in age from about nine to nineteen. Though more than one of their company were not sure his true age and had to guess at it. Some of them were orphans and lodged with the others who had family, or else in a disused cellar beside the river whence the oldest ran a part-time tailoring service.

Whereas the ruffled gentlemen and ladies alighting carriages in Baker Street about their business might have thought them paupers, they were very definitely one step higher. In their own minds the Baker Street Boys, as they affectionately referred to their own kin, were much better fixed than mere guttersnipes. They had real wages, cash money, and undertook important detective work besides the usual buying and selling, tailoring and numerous other schemes.

The oldest boy turned and called to the stragglers.

'Look lively, Barney, Jack! We better not be late. Ye know Mr 'Olmes doesn't like us to disturb 'is dinner. And I reckon that clock'll gong any moment.'

Another boy in the middle of the group turned back to see his associates lagging by fifty paces and voiced, 'The two of 'em stopped to fake a poke, I reckon. What do you say, Oliver?'

'I say, I'll peach on 'em, them and their light fingers. C'mon, faster!'

A short sprint later the group were gathered by the porch of number 221B. Their leader made a lusty effort with the bell-push and they waited, fidgeting. Then footsteps sounded behind the door and anon it opened to reveal a plump, middle-aged lady in a white apron with a purse in her hand. She had a fearsome countenance that could chase away loiterers faster than any other.

'Oh! By heaven – you took me by surprise,' she exclaimed. 'I was expecting the boy from the toyshop: he's late. I've commissioned a special gift for my great-nephew.

What do you all want anyway? Has Mr Holmes sent for you; he never said anything?'

'Beggin' your pardon, Miss, we're 'ere to see Mr 'Olmes, rightly enough, but he 'asn't sent for us. We came by our own volitions.'

'Very well, come on inside. And mind you wipe those filthy feet. I had the devil's own job last time ye came tramping through my hall.'

She led them up the staircase to the first-floor landing and knocked on the door of the apartment. A voice the boys recognised called 'Enter' and she went in before them to apologise for their unannounced visit, which was, according to her estimation, most improper especially on the eve of tea. She emerged a moment later, muttering something under her breath, bid the boys enter and tramped downstairs again.

When they came into the room they saw Mr Holmes standing by the window, looking out onto the street below. He was a tall, thin man with a pronounced forehead and stern concentration, the great part of which appeared to be taken up. He was dressed in a smoking jacket but had no pipe, only a newspaper under his arm. Oliver and his companions took off their caps and bowed themselves in great reverence. Their occasional employer spoke without facing them, but instead continued to peruse the goings-on in the street.

'Ah, Mr Dawkins and his friends! And what brings you to my apartment so close to supper? Perchance you are hungry?'

'Good evening, Mr 'Olmes, Sir, no we aint 'ungry,' the older boy replied, 'and we don't wan' a spoil your supper.'

'Forgive me, if I do not turn and face you all. I mean no disrespect. I am presently engaged in watching for a suspect and dare not leave the window. I would invite you all to sit and eat, but we can scarcely serve fourteen.'

'I thought there were twelve of us,' one boy protested in a whisper, 'or did I did me numbers wrong?'

'You forgot Mr 'Olmes and Mr Watson,' his neighbour pointed out.

'Quiet, you lot!' Oliver ordered. 'Sir, might I be so bold as to ask, who is it you is looking for? Could it be a certain, Jeremiah Coote of 'Arley Street?'

'What the − ?' Holmes spun around, aghast. 'How the devil do you know that? Speak up man! Tell me at once, do you hear?'

'Beggin' your pardon, Sir,' the boys' leader obliged, 'but we 'appened upon Mr Watson yesternoon in the park and he put us onto it.'

'Hah! So you wheedled the truth out of Watson, did you? By heaven! I shall have to get me a new associate if this keeps up, and one who is not seduced by poor boys with honest–to–God faces!'

Holmes relaxed and returned to his vigil. 'Very well, since you ask: I believe, nay, I know that Dr Jeremiah Coots is killing waifs and strays in the course of his practise. He may call it scientific research; I call it murder and I mean to catch him or, at the very least, enable Scotland Yard to get him before the year's out. The difficulty lies in the proving of it and, to that end, it would be most helpful to uncover a body. I'm sure there have been plenty of them! Alas, they are disposed of too efficiently even for me. The nearest I got was a warm grate and a pile of white ash that was too reduced to prove anything. Howbeit, I am sure I know what he's doing, as sure as I were doing it myself.'

'He burnt someone?' Jack gasped and others, too, were looking mortified.

'Yes,' said Holmes nonchalantly.

'Can't you get a warrant?' one of the boys suggested, forcefully. 'Bash his door in and scout out the place: I would.'

'The magistrate will not grant a warrant except upon sworn testimony and evidence. The fact that I know perfectly well what happened is immaterial. Furthermore Dr Coote is unlikely to leave much in the way of evidence at his practise, let alone his residence. Of course, something might have slipped his notice...'

'Sir, us lads would like to 'elp,' Oliver stated. 'And since it's almost Christmas, we'll work for 'alf-rate.'

'You would, would you?' Holmes responded.

The Baker Street Boys nodded fervently and made various comments affirming their readiness to action. Holmes sighed as the twilight outside was making his watch increasingly difficult. Shortly afterwards he gave up with the window and made his way to the fireplace. Whereupon he selected a pipe from the mantelpiece and sat down in an armchair. The boys gathered round him like children their favourite Uncle, awaiting sweets or other treats at Christmas.

'I'm not sure what you can do for me this time,' he admitted. 'I need a witness, a corpse or something else good enough for a magistrate.'

'We can follow 'im, Sir, and tell you all 'is doings,' Oliver suggested.

'But I know his doings, at least those that pertain to the case,' Holmes replied, setting a match to his pipe, 'and Lestrade is having him followed, for all the good that will do. Doubtless you could trail him with better skill than the police, but since they're on the job, Coote knows and will be all the more discreet.'

'But we're good at searchin',' one of the boys protested, ''aint we so? Didn't we find that boat for you when you asked us to?'

'Indeed you did,' he confirmed, 'in the Sholto case but, this time I think we ought to use a different tack. Pardon me the pun.'

However the boys did not understand so he made nothing of it and the discussion continued.

'Sir, why is he killing, do you know?' Young Barney was confused. The very concept of a physician who kills his charges was altogether queer to his mind. Should not the doctor heal?

A shadow passed across Holmes's face. He looked at the child, considering that one so young should hardly be subject to such evil. However, he also considered the uproar in his drawing room if he refused to answer.

'So, you are asking me to postulate a motive, are you?'

Barney and one or two of the others had no idea what the word 'postulate' meant but they nodded all the same.

'Some wretched individuals kill for pleasure – yes, truly they do, while others kill merely for expediency and still others, for gain. I think it is the middle case that applies here. 'You see, boys, Dr Coote is experimenting and many of his experiments are dangerous. What he is attempting to produce is, for the present, unknown and irrelevant in light of the fact that his subjects are dying by the cart-load.

'Of course, some people are missed more than others. Imagine, if you would, the outcry that would engulf the nation should our blessed Queen, Victoria be missing one day? The nation, nay, the whole empire would be up in arms. Now then, suppose a well-known merchant disappeared? The whole of Scotland yard would be rallied, but not the whole country. Suppose then a docker, or stoker went missing? Many people would say to themselves, Oh, well, the steamship is a dangerous beast, an occasional death is only to be expected. Lastly, suppose a beggar drowned in the sewer. Who will raise a cry for him?'

'I understand what you say, Sir,' Oliver ventured. 'Waifs and strays is disappearing and they is goin' unnoticed.'

'Precisely! But not unnoticed by me, or their Maker,' Holmes thundered. 'Boys, we shall see that scoundrel hung by New Year. Mark my words!' He paused, then said, 'Now it comes to it, I do have some work for you.'

A wave of cheer swept over the boys. This was what they came for: not the tales of death and crime, the commission, a chance to really help the cause. It made them feel on top of the world, or, at least, London.

Holmes explained, 'There is an undercover reporter doing the rounds, making enquiries of the poor. Dubious fellow indeed! Why not search him out? He is sure to pay you to keep quiet – at least until he's ready to publish.'

'What's 'is name? Has he broken the law?' Oliver asked.

'Not that I know of,' Holmes replied through a cloud of aromatic smoke. 'I know not whether he is up to good, or no good, but you will surely do yourselves good in tracking him down. Try searching in Limehouse, then go on to Spitalfields. There – I've given you a start.'

'But what's 'is name?' Oliver repeated.

'I shall not divulge his name,' Holmes insisted. 'It will be good practise for your detective work. Watson may give you an easy ride, but not me.'

'Do you think he is in cahoots with Coote?' one of the boys asked.

'That is for you to find out,' Holmes stated. 'Now, I think you ought to run along as I will be in all sorts of trouble with my housekeeper otherwise.'

Then, seeing their disappointed faces, he reached into the pocket of his jacket and handed their leader some coins, 'Here – a few extra shillings. Get yourselves a decent meal tonight. Call it an early Christmas present.'

'Thank you, Sir,' came in chorus.

Realising that their interview with the great man was at an end, the boys got up to leave. One by one they bid him 'Good evening, Sir' and filed out. Finally, as Oliver was about to close the door behind them, Holmes called him back and said, 'Dawkins! You have charge of a good crew there. Take care of them.'

'Yes, Sir,' he replied, a doleful expression on his countenance.

What rough luck they'd had. To think of it: losing a chance to hunt down a mass murderer and being asked to dodge some third-rate news correspondent. What was the world coming to?

Meanwhile back in Oxford Street, the traffic had dwindled and the toymaker was closing up shop for the night. Rex was assisting with the shutters and they were almost too much for him to bear. He swayed alarmingly on his feet as he heaved the heavy board up against the window. Whereupon his master, standing on a crate would fix the top, allowing his boy likewise to fasten the bottom. Four pitch-pine boards it took to cover the large shop window, and another for the door.

When it was done, they locked the door from the inside, drew a bar across and all was secure.

'Go to now and light the lamps, then wash those hands, quick. Mrs Arthur should have a faint if she see dirt like that!'

'Yes, Sir,' Rex replied, tired out but doing his best to be quick and obedient like a good Christian boy should.

'We shall have to deliver Mrs Hudson's present tomorrow and apologise profusely for the delay. Business can become overwhelming at this time of year. Good for the pocketbook, but *habaeus corpus!*'

'Is that why you took me on, Sir?' the boy replied, working with a brass lamp on the desk, which then flickered into flame.

'Indeed. Fancy that, my boy! A commission from Mr Sherlock Holmes's housekeeper. 'Tis but one step down from royalty.'

Rex did not understand the fervour but he dimly recognised the name of Sherlock Holmes spoken of occasionally as being some sort of would-be detective.

Chapter 4

Matchboxes and Scandal

On Sunday Rex had the afternoon to himself so he accepted an invitation from Lavender to meet her family. They met after church and although Albert would have come along too he was not permitted such liberty. So the two of them had to go without him. The Braithwaites lived about a mile or so to the south, in Field Lane, a deprived area in Clerkenwell subject to recent improvements. Whenever changes of this sort were made in the city they were always referred to as 'improvements'. In 1826 when the process began expectations were lofty indeed. It was envisaged that the changes would rank among 'the glories of the age', and that dingy alleys, dirty courts and dens of misery and squalor would be transformed into stately streets, palaces and mansions. The one oversight of this glorious vision was the question of how the poor themselves could afford to live in the lovely new dwellings provided for them.

But the problem went further back than that. From the turn of the century the population of London had grown significantly, in keeping with a general movement away from the countryside into the cities. This exodus was encouraged by the rumour that the streets of London were paved with gold and that folk could go there and make their fortune. This lie, coupled with the demolition of poor housing to make way for new factories and railway stations and other improvements meant that the poor were displaced and compressed into ever tighter and more wretched areas. While the wealthy moved out into altogether pleasanter surroundings with abundant fresh air and space.

After an half-hour walk the girl led him through a narrow entrance into a closed courtyard. Originally it consisted of stables and accommodation for servants, but was now a dilapidated shell with numerous sprawling additions, grimy outbuildings, broken windows and leaking roofs. If the landlord was receiving rent at all, he was surely not spending a penny of it on repair and maintenance. And it seemed that the residents had taken to adding their own improvements as they saw fit, making for a warren of narrow, timber-lined passageways and inadequate, cold, damp rooms. In the centre of the yard stood a brazier around which a small group of children were keeping warm, while a young woman roasted chestnuts in a pan. There was also a large copper on a brick base for hot water with a fire blazing underneath.

As they approached the throng a sudden cold draft swept around the yard bringing with it a light dusting of snow, to the delight of the younger children who rejoiced at the sight. Rex always looked forward to a 'white' Christmas and would have rejoiced with his peers but was somewhat on edge due to the reputation of the place. He likely would not have ventured into such a yard that had only one way in and out but for a guide.

Lavender spoke first to the young woman at the brazier. 'Arternoon, Mary, are they ready yet? I'm famished.'

She waved smoke out of her eyes and replied, 'They're not for you, they're for us. Whose the new togs anyway? He's not from round 'ere.'

'This is Rex, all the way from Oxford Street, if you please!'

'Blimey! To what do we owe the honner?' Mary retorted with a hint of sarcasm.

'Rex, this is Mary our neighbour and these are some of 'er young'uns, 'Arry, Clara and 'Melia, and these two are me brother and sister, Tom and Emm. Is mother at 'ome?'

'Think so,' Mary replied, scalding her fingers while testing one of the chestnuts but finding it satisfactory. 'Oi!'

Lavender snatched a chestnut and led Rex quickly across the courtyard, though a large door into what used to be a stable. Inside it had been converted into one large family room, with benches, cupboards, basin and in one corner where the manger used to be, the basket had been removed and set in a hearth. The remains of a small fire were smoking and above there was a clay chimney pipe knocked through the wall. But the hole had not been closed up well as Rex could see the sky through it. A small window had been cut into the wall facing the yard but it was wholly inadequate and the family kept the door open during the day to let in more light. The place was very dusty but what caught Rex's eye was the matter of the matchboxes – they were everywhere, in every space, including under the chairs.

Another girl was sitting working by the fire, glueing pieces of card together and then leaving them to set by the warm bricks. She looked a year or so older than Rex and barely acknowledged the two of them when they entered. Neither was she labouring at any great pace though, since the week's work was almost done, there was not any need to hurry.

'Gwen, is Mother upstairs?'

Her sister merely grunted in the affirmative but there came a 'Yes, Dear,' from above and wasting no time, Lavender beckoned Rex up a ladder into what was formerly the hay loft.

Agatha Braithwaite was thirty and the mother of five children. Her absent husband was an inveterate drinker and the family almost never saw him, which was largely to their own benefit. Of the children, Gwendoline was the eldest, then Lavender, then Thomas, then Emma and lastly the babe, who was swaddled in a basket beside the bed. The family derived a meagre income from making matchboxes, often three thousand a week but this had been a larger order for five thousand. Every Monday morning a man would visit with a box of card and glue together with a note stating the required amount. He would also take the completed matchboxes away and, subject to their quality, bring the payment the following Monday. So the wages were always a week in hand. However the Braithwaites appeared to be faring better than many of their neighbours and Rex wondered whether they were living beyond their means. He understood elementary business practice and the concepts of both credit and debt.

Ten families in all lived in the courtyard and there were but two privies for the better part of one hundred souls. And while it was common for many to exist on a diet of bread, dripping, tea and vegetables, especially in winter, that evening Rex dined on bread, jellied eels (with butter!) and fried sheep's trotters. From his point of view it was tantamount to a feast although, if truth be told, he ate well with the Arthurs too.

After supper the children had to go to bed and, as Mrs Braithwaite had an appointment, she charged her eldest with accompanying Rex home. ('It's a proper walk, and not so good after dark!') Rex thanked her for her hospitality and explained that he was perfectly ready to go home on his own, but his host insisted. So he and Gwendoline set off for Oxford Street about seven of the clock.

Rex was not careful about which way they went, his was to aim in the appropriate direction and take whichever way seemed best, avoiding the more dubious alleyways and tunnels. Gwendoline however was well aware of which streets they ought to avoid and ended up taking what he considered the long way around. But this was her patch and Rex thought it best not to argue. Then when they where about halfway to their destination, the young woman drew him aside from the road where a gentleman was alighting from a cab and paying his fare and said, 'I can take you no further. I have to go to work.'

'Don't worry, I know the way from here,' he replied. Then he added, 'Go to work, at this time?'

But she merely smiled and said, 'Good night.'

As she disappeared into the smokey darkness, he stared after her, wondering what she meant by it. Then he considered that it might have to do with a girl's nature. She was a rather queer character after all, unlike her sister who was most convivial.

The next day young Albert was that keen to hear how the previous afternoon had transpired that he even came into the shop while the master was out. Rex happily informed him of everything he had missed as they drank tankards of tea and commented on notable personages in the passing crowd. Not only this, but there was a great pile of gift-wrapped orders in the window by the tree and it made for an excellent addition to the display. The presents were stacked as high as the boys' heads and became a point of interest both for them and the many who looked in at the window.

'May I come and visit your house some time too?' Rex asked, the idea coming to him suddenly.

'I should like that,' his friend replied. Then his face fell and he became despondent.

'What is it?' Rex enquired.

'My father, he won't – we don't have visitors at our house,' he explained.

'Oh, well I suppose you're welcome here,' Rex said.

Shortly afterward Albert took up his tray, bid his friend good day and, suitably refreshed and warmed, resumed his position outside the shop selling apples. Rex closed the door after him thoughtfully. He was curious that the family refused visitors but then he considered that he had, in fact invited himself, which was considered rude in respectable circles. And who did not aspire to move in such company?

When the master arrived later he was more than a little agitated. When Rex enquired, he threw down that day's copy of the Times on the counter and remarked, 'Did I not warn thee against that detestable fellow?'

'Which fellow, Sir?' the boy asked, momentarily at a loss.

'That good-for-nought reporter! Read the headline, if you have the stomach for it, that is. I picked up the paper from the stand on my way back. The crowd around was acting the circus.'

Cautiously, Rex drew the newspaper to him, opened it and read the main headline. "Sordid City – Field Lane Prostitution. An exclusive report from our correspondent." Rex had heard the term before but was not sure what it meant though he could tell it was grievous by his master's reaction. He thought it best to read no further.

'I think I should leave it,' he confessed.

'Good Boy!' Mr Arthur replied. 'There is no need to sully yourself with that filth.' So saying he snatched up the paper and tossed it in the fire. 'That is quite enough from you, Mister Havelock Watkins-Rhymes!'

'Oh, him,' Rex said, remembering that the fellow had left his card on the counter. He scrabbled around amongst the other stationery and quickly found it. 'Has he done something terrible, Sir?'

'In the mind of all civil folk, then yes, but 'tis not for your ears. Is that his card? Cast it in the fire. We shall have no more truck with him.'

Rex hastened to obey and stuffed the card into the mouth of the stove, where it wrinkled to ash in moments.

Spurred on perhaps by previous suggestions in Letters to the Editor of their turning a blind eye to the criminal dealings within the slums, the police sprung into action the very next day and made a series of arrests. One of which involved the new acquaintances at Field Lane. However the first Rex heard of it was when Albert came tearing into the shop a few minutes past nine, without waiting for the shopkeeper to be occupied elsewhere. The moment he came tumbling through the door and the master demanded, 'What do you want, Boy?' he burst out, 'Lavender's mother's been nabbed by the traps!'

'What is that?' Rex gasped.

'Agatha Braithwaite has been arrested,' he repeated in plain English, 'it happened first thing this morn. Lavender said her ma were dragged away by a detective and two bobbies. Now the young'uns are beside their selves!'

'What about the reporter, is anyone going to arrest him?' the shopkeeper demanded.

Albert shrugged but Rex was having difficulty connecting the Braithwaites with the disgraced reporter and in the heat of the moment, thought it unwise to seek an explanation from his master. However when Albert left the shop and Mr Arthur went to confer with his wife, Rex took the opportunity and hurried outside to speak again to his friend.

'I don't really understand what's going on,' he admitted.

'Didn't you read the newspaper?' Albert rejoined. 'It told you everything.'

'No, we burnt it,' Rex said. 'The master disapproved.'

'Burnt it?'

'Yes.'

Albert frowned at him. 'So you haven't heard, you know nothing about it?' he pressed.

'About what?'

'Turns out Agatha Braithwaite is not a woman of virtue and not only that, for the past couple o' months she's been selling 'er oldest daughter too and the girl's only twelve or thirteen – which is what all the ado is about. The chap from the Times was a customer of hers. He wrote about it in the paper and that's why everyone's in uproar. Some are saying he only did it to make himself famous but if he winds up in Old Bailey he'll be more 'n that.'

'Selling?' Rex repeated. He was familiar with slavery and understood that the workhouse might pay money to a tradesman in return for his taking on an apprentice but neither of these two cases seemed to apply here.

Albert looked at him confused, as if he'd missed the point. 'Don't you know what a dollymop does?' Then Rex looked confused so his friend tried again. 'A night flower – Oh, alright – *a harlot!*'

'Oh, one of those!' Rex gulped, comprehension dawning on him. He thought about it carefully for a moment, then shook his head and replied, 'No, not really.'

'Well…' His friend reflected, and after a long pause fastened upon circumlocution. 'It's supposed to be for love, and it happens in a marriage, and sometimes before the marriage and sometimes outside the marriage. Sometimes people do it just for money, which is what the Braithwaites were up to, but, blimey! I think we should talk about this somewhere else, don't you? It's not really a subject for per-

light conversation and I'm supposed to be working, and so are you. Look!'

For his part, Rex was hardly satisfied with that answer but there was a gentlewoman entering the toyshop and he took leave of his companion and hurried in after to serve her. The finely-dressed lady, all in green with a matching hat, kept her hands in a muff and fussed over the numerous items Rex offered for her inspection. It was some test of his patience in light of the staggering events of the morning and his burning and yet unanswered questions. In the end she did not want the skittles, nor the bagatelle, nor the train set, nor the painted toy soldiers and left without purchasing anything.

And still the scandal grew. For, the day after, the talk amongst the street hawkers, who were always a valuable source of gossip, was that of a young girl eloping with a gentleman old enough to be her father. Rex was downcast when he heard them and more so when his friend arrived and confirmed his fears. Seeing Rex in distress, the apple seller gave him a bag of Coxes free.

'Father will whop me, most likely if the count is short, but you look like you need cheerin' up. *Apples! Loverly winter apples!*'

'Thank you,' Rex mumbled.

'It's all true, Gwen's run away with the same cove—'

'The reporter?'

'Exactly! The young'uns have gone to the workhouse and the babe to the parish farm, but Lavender is scared stiff of the workhouse and refusing to go. She ran away. Now another family have moved into the 'ouse she she's out on 'er ear. The neighbours can't afford to take 'er in so she's got nowhere to go.'

'Oh Lord!'

'We have to 'elp 'er.'

'I agree,' said Rex and, although he had only known her a short time, he felt a sense of duty toward her, which he could not explain. 'Will your father take her in?'

Albert shook his head. 'Not a hope,' he said firmly.

Rex then made up his mind and declared, 'I shall beg the master give her houseroom.'

'Yes, do – *do!*'

Chapter 5

A Tragic Ending

Whatever obligation Rex felt toward the girl, his friend's seemed all the greater. Indeed, he was quite taken by surprise when the apple seller unexpectedly hugged him and thanked him profusely, even becoming tearful.

For the remainder of the day Rex sought occasion to broach the subject with his master but it was not so easy. Not only was it a fearful thing to ask. He was kept busy for several hours upstairs in the workshop assembling precut wooden parts and colouring them with bright, lead paint and when they did speak, the shopkeeper was giving him instructions rather than providing a listening ear. So it was not until they were putting up the boards at five o'clock that Rex felt his chance had come.

'Master, may I beg a favour on behalf of another?'

'And what is that?' the shopkeeper asked, stepping down after fixing the last board.

Rex drew a deep breath and began, 'Sir, I have a friend who has lately become destitute. She is no slouch and grateful to work but has no where to live at present. Could we grant her shelter with us until the New Year?' He felt that limiting his request to the festive season was his best hope. The shopkeeper looked long and hard at him and for a moment it seemed to Rex as though the man agreed. However after a pause he shook his head and replied, 'I am sorry; I do not think that we can. There is scarcely room for you and you sleep under the counter. How can we take another in?'

'She can lie on the floor with me?' Rex suggested.

'No, but let her apply to the workhouse,' the shopkeeper insisted. 'If her cause is genuine she shall go and they shall take her in.'

'But the workhouse is brutal,' Rex pleaded. 'Many would rather run away and starve in a field.'

Mr Arthur shuddered and said, 'I fear that is the idea, my boy. In making the place hard, only those in genuine need will apply. I suppose their purpose is to discourage vagrants and the idle. Of course, that also means that all the rest suffer too. I wonder if the board ever considers that?'

Rex was quite disheartened but knew it was fruitless to argue. Sadly he followed the shopkeeper inside and locked and barred the door behind them. Then he swept the floor while the master cleared away and thereafter they went downstairs to supper. The same was a welcome pot of potatoes, vegetables and bags of mystery – sausages, so called because the only person who knew what was in them was 'im what made 'em.

There was scarcely talk after the meal. As was her wont Mrs Arthur retired to the corner of the room with her knitting, and judging by the size of the pullover she was halfway through, Rex guessed that she meant it for him but said not a word. Mr Arthur ventured up to the workshop to put in a precious few hours in order to keep pace with the Christmas demand. So Rex, after making up the fires and washing his hands and face, made his bed under the counter and climbed in. As he lay there and considered the dwindling number of days left until The Day, his excitement stirred and in time began to counteract the disappointment that they were not able to help Lavender

Braithwaite, the little matchstick girl as he fondly thought of her now.

His mind was intensely active, reliving Christmases past and notable events that had occurred, year by year and also gifts he had received. His previous master had been fair but presents were sparse and more often practical than pleasurable, for example boots and gloves rather than toys, games and confections. With some concentration, he was able to picture and count every Christmas back to the parish farm, or so he thought. He had no memory of his parents and knew nothing of them, and his being a foundling meant that no one else knew anything either. Of course there were rumours of prostitution and all sorts of skulduggery but in the absence of facts, speculation always abounded.

It was nearing midnight when Rex finally came by sleep, only to be woken shortly after by the chimes of the clock and then later by a faint knocking at the door, but he was so sleepy he could not perceive it and rolled over and was promptly dreaming again.

When he awoke next morning the light streaming around the edges of the shutters was unusually bright and Rex immediately hoped within himself that it signified snow! A white Christmas was always to be desired, and much better that simply a cold and wet one.

It was about a quarter before the hour they were to open, namely eight o'clock when, in addition to the usual hubbub of the street they heard distinct voices outside the shop.

'She can't be sleeping in his doorway, they'll be opening soon.'

'I seen 'er 'ere las' night, Constable an' no word of a lie.'

'Come on then, Lass, let's be having you – '

Somewhat perturbed, the shopkeeper himself went and unlocked and unbarred the door, and upon opening was confronted by a small crowd, including a police constable bending over a figure slumped in the doorway. She was an untidy tangle of shawl and blanket. When the constable gave her a firm nudge on the shoulder to wake her, she toppled over and fell across the threshold, cold and rigid as a block of ice. A fearful chill swept into the room even as those standing by gasped and the constable started, 'What the…?'

Rex had been correct in his guess about the snow. There was a thick layer in the road and on the pavement and with it the temperature had plummeted. He saw a pile of black ash in the snow beside her and the remains of a matchbox where the poor girl had tried to keep warm by burning the matches. The fleeting heat had been quite insufficient and she must have expired some time before dawn. 'Lavender?' Rex cried desperately and started forwards but the shopkeeper held him back.

The man heaved a great sigh and replied, 'Is this the dear maid you spoke of? Oh, how I wish I should have heeded you!'

'She's dead as a doornail, Sir,' the constable announced grimly, having examined the body. 'Froze to death I shouldn't wonder. Did you know her, Sir?'

The shopkeeper shook his head but Rex answered, 'She is Lavender Braithwaite, the daughter of her that was arrested in the newspaper scandal.'

'Ah – I see, well then, we cannot leave her here. If you folks will lend me a hand…'

They carried away the deceased in her own blanket and while the man and boy stood weeping in the doorway, those nearby looked on in amazement. It was a sight not often witnessed in Oxford Street and a cause of much tittle-tattle. Aside from his own grief Rex was dreading the arrival of Albert who, it could reasonably be assumed, would know nothing of the death of their friend. The shopkeeper decided to wait another hour before opening in the hope that the more impertinent amongst the crowd would lose interest gossiping to all and sundry passing by and depart.

When the apple seller arrived with his usual tray of produce however, Rex unlocked the door and hurried across the street to speak to him. Young Albert was quite devastated at the news, throwing aside his goods and collapsing against an adjacent wall, wailing with abandon and would not be comforted. Amidst the sobbing rant Rex heard particularly the boy's threat to throw himself off London Bridge. Indeed he was heart-broken and Rex was beside himself as to how to help. Finally he saw the shopkeeper opening up and had no choice but to leave the distraught where he lay.

Whether he carried out his desperate leap or not, Rex could not be sure but the apple seller was absent for the whole of the next day and for the days following. And by the weekend Rex had come to believe that the poor soul had done himself in as he promised. And all at once it became the harshest winter he had ever known. Not the threat of the rod, the hard labour or the long hours – there were none of those things here, but the grief was crushing. While working he had at least that to occupy his mind, but alone in the empty shop at night or walking the street in the snow, smoke and bitter cold, he had nothing to think on but the loss of two more friends. And although he couldn't find the words, he had invested a part of himself in each of them and as they departed, so he felt increasingly bereft. His Sunday afternoon walk turned out to be a very long one indeed and once or twice he lost his way, not paying attention to which way he had come.

The newspapers, which had been so ready to report on the scandal surrounding Lavender's family, in contrast did not print a single word concerning her demise, or perhaps they had not noticed it.

Chapter 6

Burgled!

The storm of scandal finally blew over and life returned to an even keel until two weeks before Christmas Day in the evening. Rex was tucked up in his usual place under the counter and had been unconscious of the world for about an hour. All was quiet outside and yet suddenly he awoke with a start. There was a noise: the sound of shuffling feet and hushed voices filled the room around him. From his bed he could see a sliver of lamplight coming in through the front door – it was open...? But how could that be? He distinctly remembered locking it earlier that evening. Oh not so! The shop was being burgled!

He crawled out from under his blanket, peeked over the top of the counter and gasped. A gang of about a dozen boys was in the process of carrying all the presents from the shop and loading them onto a handcart waiting outside in

57

the street. Not only had they pilfered the customers' property, they were stripping the window display as well. All at once Rex was outraged. Caring nought for his own safety, he sprang to his feet and bellowed, 'Oi! Stop that! They don't belong to you.'

The gang had not realised there was anybody else in the room and were momentarily taken aback. One or two of the younger ones panicked. They dropped what they were holding and ran out of the shop. However two of the older boys, having more presence of mind, came and caught hold of him. One of them clamped a hand over his mouth and they proceeded to bind him hand and foot and then gag him with an oily cloth. The taste of it caused him to retch and the fumes made him somewhat faint. Rex resisted with all his might, kicking out at them and writhing but they were too strong for him and soon more of them came to help their fellows. One of the older boys slapped him across the face after Rex's flailing foot caught him painfully in the kneecap.

Before long he was gripped by many hands and they dragged him into the scullery. One of them hissed, 'In the cellar with him, quick!' and they opened the door and threw him down the stairs. He flew through the dark and landed painfully, face-first in the heap of coal. There came a snort of laughter and the sound of the door being latched above him.

Immediately Rex struggled upright and tried to free his hands but they were bound tightly behind his back. He tried to rub his mouth against his shoulder to dislodge the gag but that, too, was secure. One of his assailants certainly knew his knots! Maybe he worked a barge on the river when he wasn't accessory to a crime? As he heard the gang above continuing to pilfer the toyshop, Rex crouched down and managed to reach the knot around his ankles with his fingertips. It was tricky but he untied it. With his feet free he leapt up, climbed the stairs and began kicking at the door with all his might. The noise of the gang subsided quickly after that and, half a minute later, the door was flung open and the shopkeeper standing there, a candle in one hand and poker in the other.

A look of horror passed across his face as he saw the boy bound and gagged on the stairs before him with a great red bruise across his cheek. As Mrs Arthur came down a moment later crying, 'William! William! What has happened?' he laid aside the candle and iron and proceeded to free the boy.

As soon as his mouth was clear Rex cried, 'Master, you have been robbed! A gang of boys locked me in the cellar and stole all the presents.'

At that moment a scream from his mistress in the shop confirmed the fact and the two of them hurried from the room. The door to the shop stood ajar and the night breeze was blowing in. The large pile of presents by the entrance – representing the bulk of the Christmas orders – had gone. As had the window displays and much of the goods on the shelves. Only a few items high up behind the counter remained, otherwise the place was bare.

'We're ruined,' the shopkeeper lamented, shaking his head.

Upon investigation the following morning it appeared that the burglary was committed with a certain amount of expertise – in so far as their gaining entry to the shop. No glass was broken and the door had not been forced. Therefore the culprits must have come equipped with the necessary tools as they had managed to turn the key in the lock from the outside and push it from the barrel. Thereafter, by inserting some device or other through the hole, they had managed to dislodge the bar across the door so that it fell to the ground. It was likely this noise that first caused Rex to stir.

Having gained entry it was only a matter of minutes to pilfer the goods and doubtless less time than that had not the boy disturbed them. That at least was the opinion of the constable who called at the property shortly after Mr Arthur reported the matter to the nearest police office. Mrs Arthur however had an altogether different idea. Whilst it was scarcely a case of Murder, Treason of the high affairs of State and such a private consulting detective were unlikely to entertain his powers with petty burglary, it could be hoped that Mr Holmes might be entreated of to help them. Not least because this misfortune, if left unsolved should cause dismay to a large number of innocent folk at Christmas.

The shopkeeper was rather taken up with the constable to advise his wife and even Rex doubted it would avail them, but she was quite determined upon it and set off around ten o'clock. Since there was next to nothing left to sell, Rex spent the following few hours in the workshop carefully painting a set of toy soldiers.

When he came down to lunch he was glad to see the mistress in better spirits and it transpired that in his magnanimity the detective had agreed to take her case at a nominal remuneration. To be precise: he charged a fee of one guinea. However apprehending the culprits was only a part of the resolution. Without also finding the stolen goods many of the orders would fail to be supplied, customers would demand their money refunded and it was doubtful the toyshop would continue trading in such an event.

In an effort to save the business and replenish as many orders as possible, Rex began working two more hours after supper every day while the master laboured long into the early hours, to the point that Rex was not even sure that he ever went to bed. The vigil began taking its toll as the shopkeeper became increasingly irascible. Meanwhile every night Rex retired to bed full of aches and pains and often times a sore head due to the fumes of the paint and turpentine. And even then he was kept awake by the sounds of tinkering upstairs. The one consolation was that this gargantuan effort was needed only until the twenty-fourth. Come the next morning there would be little they could do to avert whatever crisis remained.

It had persisted for a century or more within the respectable classes, the strange notion that another family could raise a child better than his own. And with peculiar regularity boys as young as ten years old were shuffled into apprenticeships in preference to being taught by their own fathers. Upon entering such an arrangement the boy commonly agreed to a ten-year servitude during which time he promised, amongst other things, not to marry. However, whatever zeal might have begotten these early commitments the long abstinence sometimes proved too much to bear and young men were known to abandon their masters and slink into taverns or other places of disrepute. There to waste away their funds on drunkenness and debauchery until they had utterly spent themselves. Whereupon, as with all Prodigals, their only hope lay in the mercy of their father.

Unlike at his previous station Rex did not enjoy the status of apprentice and, indeed, was always one outburst of temper from being on the street again. So he did his best to be as obedient and convenient as possible, especially in the fraught last few days before Christmas.

However the master's patience was about to be further tested when a deep covering of snow fell one night. By the morning the wind had blown it into drifts and many roads around them were hazardous if not quite impassable. By nine o'clock scores of workers were out clearing snow with shovels and carts and as Rex set off with a bag full of packages over his shoulder he watched the men working in the road, their breath spilling out in great billowing clouds and shovels clinking on the stones. Rex had six parcels to deliver and reckoned it would take him the better part of an hour and a half. He decided to start with the address nearest him, in Cleveland Street to lighten the load faster.

The Strand Union Workhouse in the same street was one of the earliest workhouses in London, having been built in the late 1700s on land owned by the Duke of Bedford. In those days the area was still semi-rural but had since become engulfed by the sprawling suburb. The imposing face of the four-floor, Georgian establishment with its many rows of windows and wrought-iron gates was not deceiving. The regime was desperately harsh, with over five hundred people sharing only three hundred beds and each one having half the cubic space they would have enjoyed in a London prison.

Cleveland Street had had its share of snowfall also and scores of inmates had been set to work clearing the highway. As Rex rounded the corner he saw teams of men and boys and women and girls working on opposite sides of the road, kept apart and supervised by mean-looking overseers in greatcoats and hobnail boots. It was a sorry sight compared to that in Oxford Street where those labouring were either volunteers or paid. Here the young and old alike were compelled to work in order to receive their meagre board and lodging, if indeed it qualified for such a description. Rex kept his head down and hurried past them until, about half-way along the street, he heard his name called.

'Rex!'

He turned and at once his heart leapt as he saw Albert running towards him. The young man had dropped his spade, left his fellows and raced toward his friend. Rex found himself all but knocked off his feet as Albert collided with him and embraced him wildly.

'Albert!'

'Rex, my friend, I am that glad to see you!'

'I thought you were dead,' Rex gasped, putting down his sack, 'after hearing you threaten so.'

However they had not long to speak as an overseer had already barked some incoherent order in their direction and was making his way toward them, lash in hand. Albert was looking pale and ill and Rex caught hold of his arm, picked up the sack and whispered, 'Come, run away with me, I shall save you. You and me can outrun that brute.'

However his friend shook his head. 'No, but tell your master to purchase me for his apprentice. The workhouse is overcrowded and the board shall be only too pleased to release me for five pounds.'

The next moment the overseer was upon them and without quarter the whip cracked through the air. Albert smarted as it stung him around the neck and the tip curled around and cut Rex across the cheek.

'Mind that whip, Sir, or my master shall have you up for assault! I am not your prisoner!' Rex snapped.

'Be off with you then,' the man roared, 'and you, Cummins, get back to work!'

And as Rex dabbed his cut angrily with the sleeve of his coat, Albert allowed himself to be dragged by the collar back to his place at the side of the road. And no matter how unjust it was, the discovery that his friend was not dead was a joy to him, and after watching for another minute, Rex continued on his way. So the workhouse was overfull? Well, that was no surprise but Albert was also correct, they would readily let him go to make space, especially in the case that one were insubordinate and Rex had a feeling that his friend was. Maybe that was why the man had used the lash without notice?

He found the address he was seeking a short distance up the road – an elegant townhouse with a wreath of holly strung about the shining black door. Rex opened his sack, took out the parcel, made his way up the short flight of steps and knocked. The lady who answered the door was the very same who had declined to purchase anything when she visited the toyshop. So she had bought something after all. Maybe she was too proud to deal with a boy and after viewing the stock had sent a servant in the days following? Rex handed her the parcel, received the balance of the payment and bid her good day. Then he set off for his next delivery.

After the trials and tribulations of recent days, finding Albert to be alive instead of dead lifted Rex's spirit wonderfully and he was so happy, he barely noticed the long, hard walk in the cold. All along the way the question on his mind was whether he dare beseech his master on behalf of another worthy cause. The light of his hope was that the master, being greatly affected by the death of the girl, might be moved to help the boy. Howbeit their present circumstances were distressed already and how could they manage with another. Then he considered that Albert had already worked and could make deliveries as easily as he. So why could he not earn his keep also? Still, the matter would need to be delicately handled.

Rex returned to the shop with a spring in his step and when the shopkeeper looked up from his work he could not but notice.

'A strangely merry countenance I see?'

'Master, 'tis Christmas after all,' Rex replied, placing the empty sack on the counter and handing over the proceeds.

'If ye have good tidings share with all,' the shopkeeper insisted. 'Were our customers overgenerous?'

'Oh, not that,' Rex explained cheerfully, pulling off his coat. 'I have just seen alive a friend I lately thought dead: Albert Cummins.'

'Do I know him?' the master replied, counting the money into the box.

'Yes, he is the fruiterer's boy. He was clearing the road with the workhouse crew in Cleveland Street.'

'Why has he left his father's business?' Mr Arthur asked, intrigued.

'I did not ask him,' Rex admitted. 'Perhaps because he was distraught at Lavender's death and preferred not to return home?'

'Bah! Children cannot feel such attachment or grief at the loss of those that are no kin.'

'Master,' Rex protested, 'said you not yourself how dire is life in the workhouse? And don't I know it right well! Why ever then would a boy seek refuge there if he were not sorely stricken?'

The shopkeeper closed the lid of the box with a snap and looked up, taken aback.

'Maybe – ' he said thoughtfully.

Rex was wondering whether he ought broach the subject there and then but as he wavered the moment passed and the pressing concerns of business prevailed.

While the mistress took a turn at the counter, the master and his apprentice retired to the workshop for several hours. The majority of the work involved replacing that which had been lost and new orders were set aside. Mr Arthur reckoned it better to disappoint customers rather than not deliver what they had already paid for. The only advantage in this was that, having previously assembled, painted and packed the same items, Rex knew well what he was doing and was able to work with more speed.

Luncheon consisted of bread and dripping while they worked and afterwards, around two o'clock Rex set off with another sackful of presents. This round would encompass several miles and he did not expect to be back before supper. His first delivery was in nearby Wimpole Street, then he had two more in Harley Street and finally he had to venture all the way out to Pentonville where he had three more parcels to deliver. They tried to group the orders together by area but even so, there was still a considerable amount of walking involved. Of course he could always take a cab but that would eat into their earnings so he preferred to go on foot.

Chapter 7

The Villainous Dr Coote

The evening smog was descending and the fume of it made him cough frequently. And now having delivered his last package – to Mrs Albright – Rex was keen to return to the shop, the consolation of supper and a warm bed in front of the range. His master had been talking about his sleeping on the scullery floor, which would certainly bring its advantages. One of these with it being winter, where he would keep a small fire going all night, not just for comfort's sake but to expedite breakfast the following morning. Despite the recent upset of such a terrible loss, the shop would continue trading and, who knew whether next year would make up for it?

The traffic rattled past him as he walked. Lively talk and music sounded from a tavern, some drunken impertinence outside and seasonal merriment apparent everywhere. Yes, Christmas was here.

Nearing Oxford Street, he turned down an alleyway, shivered slightly in the cold and sped up. No sooner had he done so, than a hand shot out from a dark doorway and caught him about the collar.

'What the – ?'

And before he knew what was happening, Rex found a hand clamped over his mouth and himself dragged inside the building. He struggled but to no avail. The man pulling him was strong and quick about his business.

Almost paralysed with fear, Rex found himself half dragged, half carried up several flights of stairs in the darkness. All the way his mind played tricks with him, except that the play was very real. Lately he had heard the costermongers speak of children disappearing off the street but had paid little heed to their rumours. Life in the slums was such that had it not come to be accepted as a part of living in a great city? Very few complaints made their way to the police office and fewer still were acted upon. Indeed there was more than one magistrate that would sooner commit a child to three months hard labour than to order a search be made for him.

Yet the rumours were true and now he knew it! When they reached the top of the stairs a shaft of light streamed through a small, broken window. The assailant, dressed head to toe in a heavy, velvet cloak turned into a room and deposited Rex onto a couch.

Pained and breathing desperately fast, Rex stared up at him, furious and afraid in equal measure. Meanwhile the man lit a lamp on the mantelpiece before turning to his quarry. His eyes were keen but his face largely obscured by a handkerchief. So he pulled it down and spoke.

'Wait there,' he said, 'while I prepare your board and lodging!'

Whoever the fellow was, his conversation was that of a gentleman and Rex was taken aback, expecting to be roughly addressed by someone of his own class. Certainly it was difficult to equate these manners with this manhandling.

'I need no board and lodging,' the boy protested. 'Who are you, Sir?'

'Jeremiah Coote, Doctor of Medicine,' the man replied and he left the room without further comment, closing the door behind him and locking Rex inside.

A doctor? 'Twas a strange thing indeed that a doctor should snatch a boy off the street, Rex thought to himself. And why should a stranger offer him board and lodging when he had no need of such? He had heard of Thomas John Barnardo who was reputed to help those in want. Could this fellow be a colleague? Rex looked about the room and perceived by the poor light of the lamp that it might once have been an office of some sort. There was a desk by a window and volumes of ledgers on a shelf.

He was sore from being hauled up the stairs and wondered why indeed the man should be so rough if hospitality were his true intention. It made no sense.

About five minutes later Coote appeared again and bid him come through into the next room. Rex obliged and found himself in the large, open space of what he now realised was a warehouse. Though it was mostly empty; there were a few barrels and boxes stacked in rows but not much else. At the far end of the room there were two, large loading doors open to the night, through which they would bring the goods. Outside a block and tackle ran through a gin wheel suspended from a wooden beam.

'Here – ' Coote indicated a makeshift surgery in the furthest corner of the room.

Rex looked and saw two beds – one of them occupied – and a table with scientific equipment.

'You should rest now and in the morning, enjoy the best meal of your life,' the man said. 'Come, lie down.'

Rex was obeying his instructions by dint of the fact Coote was an adult and a medical practitioner, but was very much puzzled and disturbed. The man was tall, dark-haired and slim. He had a certain zeal about his countenance, penetrating eyes and spoke smoothly as though to reassure. But Rex had acquaintance with those of the street and, accordingly, a keen sense of his own survival.

He glanced at the boy in the bed opposite, who appeared a few years younger than himself. He was lying on his back under the sheet quite still, looking at Rex. But he was very still, too still, and his eyes were open wide – like a warning! Rex looked to see if he could detect the boy's chest moving. He could not... Rex now understood that the lad beside him was dead and that he would be too, unless he acted very quickly indeed.

With a great effort he managed to keep his expression easy as Coote, smiling warmly, bid him lie down and get comfortable while he prepared a 'sedative' to 'help rest' him. In the few moments while the man's back was turned, a panic surged through Rex such as he'd never known, along with a savage determination to save his life at any cost. He knew not who this fellow was, but if killing were his pleasure, here was one who would fight back.

Coote turned with a syringe in his hand and told him not to fear a small prick. ('A girl might swoon but I expect better of you'.) Then, as he came close, Rex pushed his hand away suddenly and Coote stabbed himself with the needle and cried out.

'Ah! Damn you! Imbecile – you have infected me!' He roared and would have brained him there and then but was anxious to suck the preparation from the wound.

Coote was between him and the stairs and Rex knew the only way out was through the loading doors. He sprang up, ran around the bed and sprinted across the room, Coote in pursuit, sucking his left hand. As he neared the doors, Rex remembered they were several floors up and could only make one, feeble plan of escape in his mind.

He burst through the doors and jumped off the ledge, gripping the rope at the same time. A bare yard behind him, Coote emerged and lunged at his collar. Rex swung out, away from the doors and downwards as the rope rattled through the wheel and the heavy block and hook rose up on the other end.

In his zeal Coote was unable to save himself. With a great cry, he toppled off the ledge and fell headlong to the ground three floors below. He landed face-down with a sickening thud.

Moments later the block jammed in the wheel and the rope was almost wrenched from Rex's grasp. He cried out in pain as it cut him but managed to keep a hold. And he came to a halt dangling in mid-air at about the level of the first floor.

He felt his grip beginning to wane and wondered desperately what to do next. His escape from death, being possibly only a temporary reprieve, and the apparent retribution on the head of Coote meant little to him now, if he also should fall. The street below was a drop of twelve feet in his estimation. Should he risk letting go? He was sure he could survive if he landed upright, but not without some injury. He reckoned a broken bone or two was the minimum he could expect. Those cobbles looked awfully hard at this distance, both implacable and uneven.

The cold night air made him shiver alarmingly and his grip began to weaken further. Then an idea came to him.

He soon found that by kicking his legs, he could swing back and forth on the rope. It took a little time to perfect the rhythm but soon he was gathering momentum and, before long, he managed to swing himself into the first-floor doorway. Whereupon he caught hold of the reveal and dropped down onto the wall.

He let go the rope and balanced on the ledge, which was barely a foot wide. He tried the doors but found them locked. After a moment to gather his thoughts, he considered that the only way down from here was to lower himself from the ledge. He estimated the drop to be six to eight feet – easy enough for a lively lad.

So, bracing himself, he sat on the ledge, turned and lowered himself to arm's length. Then he shut his eyes and let go. A second later he landed uncomfortably on his hindquarters but was relieved to feel no significant harm.

He got to his feet and made his way over to the body lying in middle of the road. Coote was spread-eagled, his face staved in. It was a ghastly sight. Rex wondered whether he should alert the authorities, but how could he explain things without his being charged with murder? As one of his former colleagues had once pointed out, "they're so very keen on hanging folk these days".

Suddenly a Hansom cab driving furiously appeared around the corner at the far end of the road. Not wanting to face the repercussions, Rex ran for his life, heading down the nearest alley.

An hundred yards in he met a dead-end and scolded himself for his folly. Of course, this was the mews of the big houses on street. He should know the area better than this by now, surely? It was his own neighbourhood after all. The mews, he thought – heavens! That meant stables and coal cellars. Why, there should be a score of hidey-holes in a place like this!

He heard the cab clatter to a halt some way off and began searching desperately for a suitable place to conceal himself. Then he hit upon the cover of a large coal hole. He knelt down and began scrabbling for a handhold. Finding the edge, he heaved with all his might. Thankfully it had been opened recently and moved easier than it could have done.

Rex slid the heavy iron ring aside and lowered himself carefully into the dark hole. He was not sure of the drop, but six inches later he landed on what was unmistakably a heap of coal. But there was also something else – something utterly unexpected. Something that twinkled in the moonlight and crushed more easily than coal. What on earth…?

It took a good few minutes for his eyes to adjust to the gloom but then, emerging like long-lost treasure in the depths of a pirates' cave, boxes, boxes colourfully wrapped of all shapes and sizes – presents! Christmas presents! The stolen Christmas presents; he had inadvertently found the whole lot of them, it seemed. But, by what strange magic were they here, of all places?

The shock was greater than anything that had happened to him this night. Rex almost fainted. In the end he just sat there, his mind reeling at the turn of events. Then he heard footsteps approaching in the alley. Two men by the sound of it but, before he could think what to do, there was a commotion at the entrance above and then the tall figure of a man lowered himself through the hole. Rex pressed himself into a corner and froze.

'Pass me a light, Watson, there's a good chap.'

Someone above then passed down a carbide lamp and immediately the cellar was full of light. Rex squinted in the sudden brightness.

'Well, I never – ! And who might you be, young Master?'

'My name – ' he faltered ' – my name is Rex, Sir.'

'My name is Holmes, Sherlock Holmes,' he replied.

'The Sherlock Holmes?' Rex gasped, breathlessly.

'Indeed,' Holmes replied, extending a hand. 'Pleased to meet you.'

However Rex didn't take his hand. Not out of rudeness, in fact, he did nothing else of his own volition. Instead, after muttering something quite incomprehensible, he fainted.

Chapter 8

Albert's Fate

He came round in the front room of the toyshop surrounded by a group of adults. The first thing he perceived were their concerned voices and when he opened his eyes, there were expressions of relief and thanksgiving. He was lying on the table on soft cushions. Beside him were Mr and Mrs Arthur, a police inspector, a constable and Sherlock Holmes. A middle-aged man was also present whom, although he did not know him, Rex assumed must be Dr Watson. After all, the man had what looked like a medical bag and who hadn't heard of the private investigator and his colleague?

The presents had apparently been retrieved from the cellar, some worse for wear and others squashed, and were stacked in a pile just inside the door.

'Aha! The boy is awake,' Holmes remarked as Rex sat up. 'Did I not say, have no fear, Madam?'

'The boy swooned, that is all,' Holmes's companion asserted, 'nervous exhaustion if you ask me.'

Mrs Arthur made no reply but simply hugged Rex and wept for joy.

'I found the presents,' he explained, 'and that man, Dr Coote, he's dead. He fell from the top floor of the warehouse.'

'Yes,' the inspector rejoined, 'we'd like to ask you some questions about that.'

'No need, inspector,' Holmes interceded. 'I can vouch for the boy. You know as well as I there's an infamous trail of dead infants behind Coote. The man was quite insane, you know. He must have accosted Rex in the street and would have done him in, just as surely he did the other poor wretch. But Rex, here, escaped his clutches, didn't you?'

'Yes, Sir.'

'Good lad! And to cap it all, not only did you get to Dr Coote before I did, you also found the stolen presents before me. You know, I may have to consider my position. It seems I have competition.'

Rex was not sure how to answer that. He thought it would be churlish to point out that he hadn't in fact been seeking Dr Coote so instead he asked, 'Mr Holmes, Sir, have you any idea who it was that stole the presents?'

'Aha, as to that, I am afraid I do,' he replied with a hint of forlorn.

'Who was it?' the inspector snapped, pulling out a notebook and pencil.

'My very own Baker Street Irregulars, that is to say, Oliver Dawkins and his friends. Of all the insults!'

'Great Scott!' Watson barked.

'Dawkins and Co? I thought they worked part-time for you, Mr Holmes?' the inspector remarked.

'They did on occasion until recently, I fear. It seems they thought ill of my latest commission and decided to return to their old ways.'

'Good Lord! They shall have to answer for it, and not just the burglary,' the inspector warned, considering Rex again, 'but the assault too.'

'Indeed they shall!' the detective agreed. 'However the hour is late and duty calls. So I shall take my leave and bid you all a Merry Christmas!'

By the time Rex got to bed it was nearing midnight and yet the excitement of the evening threatened to keep him from precious sleep for many hours. It had been enough to turn any boy's head: finding his friend alive, being abducted, finding the stolen presents and meeting the great detective all in one day! After that even Christmas Day itself might appear dull in comparison.

The next few days were the busiest the toyshop had ever known. The greater part of the salvaged parcels were undamaged and needed only the coal dust brushing off. Some had to be repacked and a few replaced altogether – those that Rex had landed on. And whatever the Baker Street Boys had meant to do with them, their plans had come to nought. It was perhaps one of the stupidest crimes to commit, to personally affront Mr Sherlock Holmes and several of the older members of the gang had already been apprehended and charged. Oliver Dawkins had thus far evaded capture and was reputed to be in hiding.

In view of the need to for speed, Rex took a cab loaded with sacks of presents and made twenty or thirty deliveries each day, prompting some comment about his being the shade of St Nicholas in his youth.

And at last the great effort was complete, with three days to go. It was a Saturday and they closed the shop at noon to give themselves a day and a half to recover. The one piece of unfinished business was for Rex to ask his master whether they could take in Albert as another help. And to do so in time for Christmas would be perfect in Rex's mind. He had no idea how swiftly the workhouse might complete the transaction, especially as Monday would would be the twenty-fourth and the magistrates, like everyone else would be looking to go home early.

He took his chance after supper that evening as they sat at the table and talked.

'Master can I beg a favour?' he began nervously.

'Ask away,' the shopkeeper replied jovially. His relief that all things had been saved made him as light and well-disposed as a nip of gin after a good meal.

'My dear friend Albert is ill-treated in the workhouse in Cleveland Street and I was – ' he faltered ' – I was hoping we might bring him here to live and work. He is used to trade and could serve thee well.'

The shopkeeper looked at him with a strange expression upon his face. Meanwhile Mrs Arthur voiced, 'Nay, child, you have been very good but we cannot take in another. We have scarce enough as it is.'

'And I might have said the very same,' her husband agreed. Then he looked again at Rex and added, 'but the last time I refused this boy's request there was a dead child on my doorstep the very next morning! I can never countenance that again.'

Mrs Arthur protested, 'William, we cannot; we have not the room.'

'We shall manage if need be,' he replied. 'What say you, shall we give the lad a Christmas?'

'Yes, please,' Rex rejoined. 'The workhouse will release him for five pounds.'

'Fair enough, then I shall go Cleveland Street on Monday morning and enquire after him,' the shopkeeper concluded.

'Oh, thank you, Master,' Rex said, springing up and hugging the man.

It was somewhat to the ire of the mistress but she graciously said nothing and proceeded to clear the table.

Rex was fidgety with excitement for the remainder of the day and unable to settle to anything. This was especially true for the Sabbath and the two hours the following morning while the master was away to the workhouse. Yet Mr Arthur returned with Albert in tow just before midday and the boy was beaming. He and Rex embraced upon meeting and Rex began telling his friend excitedly all the things he hoped they could do.

'Make not too many plans,' Mr Arthur warned them. 'I have only agreed a two-week trial with the board! Payment is upon approval.'

'Sir, I'll work my 'ands raw for you,' Albert vouched.

The boy had with him one small bag containing the sum of his worldly goods, which did not include a change of clothes. However, as he and Rex were about the same size, Rex gladly offered some of his own. It was agreed that the two of them should sleep on the scullery floor on the conditions they stole no food and kept the grate hot all night. That evening they laid two straw mattresses near the hearth and then the master and mistress retired.

Rex finished washing his hands and face and turned just as his friend was pulling a dirty grey nightshirt over his head. For a brief instant, in the lamplight Rex glimpsed all manner of bruises, burns and injuries on Albert's back and shoulders. Without managing to prevent himself he gasped out, 'Al, what's that?'

Albert, who perhaps, being used to sleeping alone had momentarily forgotten he was in company, span around and, looking awkward, replied, 'Oh, just a few scratches.'

But his attempt to brush the matter off as unimportant did nothing to diminish his friend's concern. Rex came over to him with the lamp in hand and said, 'Let me see.'

Albert shrugged him off and said, 'No, I'm tired, let's get some rest.'

Rex, however would not be dissuaded. 'Let me see or I shall call the master.'

So Albert relented. 'Oh, very well, then.' He pulled up his shirt and allowed Rex to examine the marks on his back closely by the lamplight. There were numerous welts, scars and one or two fresh cuts and bruises. This was no mere discipline; Albert was evidently the victim of battery and had been for some time.

Rex called to mind the Hebrew slaves and their cruel taskmasters. 'Cor lummy!' he exclaimed, 'who did this to you, the workhouse?'

Shaking his nightshirt down again Albert said, 'Only the recent ones. No, it was my father. He takes "spare the rod" very keenly. I 'ate to speak against 'im but the man's a bit of a tyrant.'

'So that is why you would not let me come to your house?' Rex ventured.

His friend nodded.

'And why you ran away to the workhouse?'

Albert did not answer. Instead he merely grunted and settled himself under his blanket.

'I am so sorry.'

Rex blew out the lamp and he too climbed into bed and threw a blanket over himself. He wriggled about to get comfortable in the straw and then rolled over towards the red glow of the grate. It was solace to feel the warmth on his face. From his point of view it was a season of triumph; not only the saving of the stolen goods but the rescue of his friend too. And yet, at the same time he felt no different than before. He had simply worked to survive after losing his apprenticeship.

With it being the most auspicious night of the year they both suffered a rather fretful sleep and when the clock chimed midnight, found themselves awake again.

'Happy Christmas! I wonder if I'll have any presents,' Albert mused.

'We are living in a toyshop!' Rex whispered, urgently. 'Here are all the presents you could want. Happy Christmas!'

And with that they slept.

Chapter 9

The Abandoned

Mr and Mrs Arthur must have put in many hours the boys were unaware of as, overnight a transformation took place. A tree had been erected in the scullery, in keeping with the fashion popularised by the Royal Family. Sprigs of holly were festooned on the tops of cupboards and shelves with peas dipped in red wax to resemble berries. And two small piles of presents appeared at the foot of each bed. Upon waking Rex's first thought was that he was still asleep, then he imagined he had awoken in some grotto, or else a shop window display.

Albert was thrilled with the presents and Rex had the fleeting impression that his friend was not used to receiving them. Without considering that the master and mistress had laboured long into the night to bring about such a decorative change and were likely needing to sleep late, the boys sprang up and began tearing at the packages. Rex had a box of confectionery, fruit, a cake, a pair of new shoes and a pencil and ledger. Ah, bookkeeping, he thought wryly, perhaps the master was wanting him to practise keeping his own records from now on? Meanwhile Albert had also received fruit and a cake, together with a set of toy soldiers and a pullover, which Rex had a suspicion had been meant for someone else but said nothing. He merely smiled at his friend's joy and when Albert slipped it on, commented that he looked every bit as though his ship had come in.

When it occurred to Rex that they ought to be considerate, he bid his friend quiet down and suggested they get dressed, put the kettle on the stove and make breakfast.

'I can't cook,' Albert whispered.

'It's easy enough,' Rex explained, clearing away the wrappings, 'we can fry everything. You fetch the water and I'll stoke the fire.'

A bowl of sugar mice and a plateful of nuts lay on the table, which they had not noticed, being taken with the gifts. So they abandoned cooking and decided to sustain themselves on these instead, washed down with a lukewarm jug of wassail punch they found on the stove. They both drank a little too much and Rex had a headache for the next few hours. Nonetheless the two of them had the run of the place until the mistress came downstairs at about eleven o'clock. To her fortune Rex had heard noises upstairs prior and already had a large pot of tea brewing in readiness.

'Bless you! Merry Christmas,' she said, as he passed her the beverage in her favourite cup.

'Thank you very much for the presents, Ma'am,' he obliged.

'Yes, indeed,' Albert agreed, nodding vigorously. 'It's the first time – anyway, thank you, Ma'am.'

Nothing more needed to be said and Mrs Arthur simply smiled, no doubt pleased that her significant overnight effort had been well received. It turned into a very easy, an almost lazy day. Mr Arthur would, out of habit and deep conviction, have attended church on Christmas morning, as would they of his household. However, due to the their late rising, they had missed the service. Breakfast was taken at lunch time, and luncheon at dinner time. And afterwards Rex felt he needed to walk off his food. So Albert offered to show him his own house and, with their master's approval, they put on hats and coats and set off shortly before six o'clock.

The street, which had been quiet all day, had returned to something like it's usual noisiness. There were a small number of folk taking in the air, such as they could get and a carriage or two thundered up the road.

'Follow me!' Albert said, leading the way.

After a brisk walk it became apparent to Rex that they were heading towards Clerkenwell. When he queried this, his companion remarked, 'Oh, yes, my place is quite nearby the Braithwaites'. Father 'as a shop on the main road, rather like your place.'

A heavy mist was swirling around the wintery streets and the gas lamps were flickering vainly in an effort to light their way. Rex surveyed the road before them and saw the form of a young woman beside a lamp at the crossroads. He could not tell why his attention was drawn to her.

'Almost there, another five – ' Albert stopped and stared. 'I don't believe it!' he cried, incredulous. 'Gwen?'

And with that he ran towards the lone figure up ahead. The young woman appeared to be waiting beneath the streetlamp. Rex hurried after him and as they drew closer, to his utter shock and surprise he recognised the elder

Braithwaite daughter. Conspicuous in spite of the drifting fog, she was wearing a dress that was somewhat immodest and wrapped tightly in a shawl. She turned as they approached and the two boys skidded to a halt in front of her. Unexpected as they were, she seemed much the less moved and alarmed than they.

'Oh, 'allo Albert.'

'Gwen, are you alright? I heard you 'ad eloped,' he gasped.

'Keep your voices down,' she hissed. 'I'm fine. 'Allo Rex. You two out on the town, then?'

The door of the inn opened behind them at that juncture and a group of men spilled out, some worse for wear in drink. They caught a snatch of a sea shanty, raucous voices and a harmonica. Then the door closed again.

'What happened to you? The newspaper said—' Rex began earnestly.

'I know,' she interrupted. 'The plan was we should elope, but the scandal grew too big for 'im and 'e walked out on me. The coppers want a talk to 'im but 'e's run off to Bristol so I 'eard, 'e mentioned 'e 'ad friends there.'

'I am sorry,' Rex commiserated. 'What are you doing here? Have you a place to stay?'

'Are you working?' said Albert, scowling at the men across the road who had emerged from the inn. They were standing around talking, though their conversation was seemingly as incomprehensible to themselves as to others.

'A girl's gotta live 'ain't she?' Gwen protested. 'I rent a room nearby.'

Rex turned to his friend. 'Have you any money?' he said, digging his hand in his pocket and pulling out a shilling.

'What are you like!' Gwen scorned.

Meanwhile Albert produced only tuppence. Rex took it and offered both coins to the young woman. 'Here, take it,' he said.

'Don't be silly,' she scolded, 'you're too young for that!'

'And you weren't?' Albert retorted. 'Anyway, he doesn't want that, he wants to help – I think.'

Rex nodded. 'Take this and go home,' he said urgently. 'I can't save you from this life but have one night of peace on us, if nothing else. Come on, it's Christmas Day.'

And when it became clear they were buying her a night off the street her face cracked and she sniffed and wiped away a tear. She took the proffered money gladly and said,

'You're a good boy, Rex, don't you ever change!' Then she hugged him and kissed him on the cheek.

'Don' I get a kiss then?' Albert baulked.

'Not you, you little shaver! But thanks for the tuppence anyhow.'

Just then a broad fellow in a sailor's coat approached and asked, 'I wonder whether you can help me tonight, my love?'

'Sorry, Guv'nor, I'm off 'ome,' she said bluntly. 'G'night boys!'

And smiling, she turned and marched away, leaving the man standing there bewildered in the lamplight while two of his mercantile colleagues across the street mocked and whistled at his frustration. He might have vented his anger on the boys but they had not stayed there to find out.

'Gwen, wait!' Albert called, marching after her down a narrow alleyway. 'Don' you want t' 'ear our doings? How long 'ave you been back? Did you 'ear about your poor sister?'

She stopped halfway down the alley and turned sharply. 'What about 'er? Run away from the work'ouse?'

Rex and Albert looked at one another, aghast.

'She doesn't know,' the former whispered frantically. It was a horrifying thought indeed. However were they going to break the news of Lavender's death to her?

'What are you two whisperin' about?' she demanded.

'You tell 'er,' Albert hissed.

The distress Rex had hoped to spare her for the night was nothing in comparison to the tragic news of Lavender's demise. And for one whose mother had recently been thrown in jail and whose sister was dead, Gwen was strangely unmoved, as though she had no capacity either for pleasure or pain. Rex could not understand it but, in hindsight, he supposed many children would grieve over the loss of both parents, while he himself barely considered the matter. For him it was simply a fact of life, like rich and poor, old and young, honest and corrupt. So maybe he and she had something in common?

After escorting her back to her lodging Albert had little interest in showing Rex his own home but agreed to in spite of his feelings. In the end he walked quickly past the place on the other side of the and, after pointing it out, refused even to stop.

Rex glanced up at the shop, with accommodation above and two large doors leading to a warehouse beside it.

The sign over the doors was the very same as that on the tray: Edwin Cummins and Co. Fruiterers.

After brooding over the establishment for a minute or two, Rex caught up with his friend who was waiting for him fifty yards up the road by a postbox.

'I'm never going back,' Albert said as they set off for home.

'That bad, was it?' Rex could only guess at his friend's sufferings.

'It was only my – ' he hesitated ' – my friendship with Lavender that kept me going, I reckon. Now she's gone I've got nothin' 'ere, only bad memories. So I'll stay with you if I can.'

Chapter 10

Inheritance

The recovery of the stock meant that the toyshop was able to fulfil its entire order book and they were even left with a small surplus, which Rex suggested distributing to the poor, but Mr Arthur wanted to use to replenish the shelves and window display. Thus the future of the business was secure although the adventure of the preceding few weeks had left them feeling rather windswept, and their nerves not a little tried. The boys had fun taking down the decorations on the sixth and cutting up the tree and burning it in the stove. It made for a roaring blaze as the pine oil burned very hot.

As with many shops the festive season was when they made enough sales to keep them through the following months when trade generally dropped off. This lull meant less work and more time for repairs and maintenance. It also provided time for reflection, and consideration of the future.

Albert had proved himself a lively lad and when Mr Arthur understood his unpleasant situation at home, he duly took him on as apprentice, giving the young man the security and comfort he had lacked prior to that. Of course there was more to the job than mere selling, there was the work involved in making the toys, and that required a certain amount of skill and craftsmanship, something which could not be acquired in a short time. There was also the bookkeeping. Albert agreed readily to a five-year term, renewable thereafter by either party. They even drew up an agreement and signed it. Though Albert's education was somewhat lacking and Rex undertook to school him to better his reading, writing and arithmetic.

Rex was joyful that his friend had become the shopkeeper's apprentice but in relation to his own career, things had been rather silent. And although the Arthurs had shown no hint of their disapproving of him, Rex began to wonder whether his services may yet be dispensed with. Then, one Sunday afternoon, as he and Albert were about to take the air, his master called them back and invited them to sit.

'Now then, Rex,' Mr Arthur began, 'as you know, when Mrs Arthur and I took you in we were unsure as to how long we should need you and, indeed, whether we should keep you. Well, here we are in the New Year and, I must say, it has been something of an epiphany. You have shown Mrs Arthur and me the true meaning of Christmas and for that, we are greatly indebted to you; more than we can say. And we feel our part would not be fulfilled without some further action. Thus we have prepared the necessary papers for your adoption, if you will consent to live with us. What do you say?'

'Adoption? Why, Sir, Miss! I am beside myself with this wonderful gift. And what of Albert? What shall become of him?'

'We shall keep him on as apprentice as agreed and, in due course when we retire, the two of you may have care of the shop yourselves.'

'You're givin' the toyshop to us?' Albert replied, astounded.

'Not yet, young master! Not until I've had five good years labour out of the two of you, and more than likely seven.'

'Cor lummy,' Albert gasped.

Meanwhile Rex said nothing, as he was feeling quite faint.

Five years later the two young men stood and watched in awe as the signwriter finished his work with one last flourish. And when he climbed down and took away the ladder, the bold, yellow letters read Arthur Rex and Cummins Bespoke Toys and Gifts. The two friends were well pleased and they shook hands and went back inside the shop.

Printed in Great Britain
by Amazon

75287833R00066